THE PROMISE ©

The dark hole is still silent

How have you been my soldier?

I look calm inside still turbulent

Have been begging the molder

To take away the torment

I miss you darling

I am standing at the pinnacle

Where we used to hide

Seems like I expect a miracle

Of your kiss from the side

There is the silence of a tabernacle

I miss you darling

Hey Norman

I brought our son along

He is now a grown man

He seems to be singing a song

Gosh! The resemblance of human

You have been gone for long

I miss you darling

Last month he turned ten

I told him to make a wish

He said 'I wanna be daddy or BenTen'

Put off the candles left the ash

He didn't look ten

It was you that I saw or so was my wish

I miss you darling

Our mother is growing old too fast

I know she bleeds inside

I always think of her first

The grandson always on her side

Tell her not to fail the test

By leaving us behind

Tell her it's too early to rest

We miss you darling

She dreams louder at night

Calls your late father

It gives me a fright

Each day she is going further

Her conversations slight

I look in her eyes and call her mother

She sheds tears seems to be in a fight

We miss you darling

Tell father we don't want to be alone

Tell him to stop calling mum

We will be shattered if she be gone

Although she is often mump

Without her we will be forlorn

Norman, we desperately need mum

I miss you darling

Norman I am so scared

World is crashing under my shoulder

All the people I revered

Are now a shredder

Their dignity life has battered

They should behave older

By their innuendos I am not flattered

To raise our son I will be bolder

They are shameless including reverend

I miss you darling

Look at our baby

Isn't he adorable?

'I love you mummy' is his hobby

Just like you he is amiable

He is waving at us hubby

His heart is noble

He is coming

I miss you

"Mummie, we have to go

It was long ago

But I know you miss daddy

Have sung a song for him too

Do not shed a tear

I came to give him the promise

That I will take care of you

Hug me mum

Grandma is alone

Join be aboard

C'mon, let's go mum'

He is right

We've got to go

See you Norman

I miss you darling

BITING BETRAYAL ©

Two soldiers left for the war

Left their betrothed in the cold

Not to lay a whore they swore

Not to have their Morals sold

Promised to be true to the core

Judas kissed his betrothed

Samson had no one to kiss

His betrothed was in the house

He envied his friend

As they moved towards the ice

The soldiers fought the fierce war

That left their feet sore

They remembered the promises

The weddings waited

Their bed duties omitted

The brides had promised
To boldly bare the biting cold
Their lips unkissed
Their pillows unoccupied
Their hearts in the war
Where the soldiers were
Promised not to be laid

It was the worst of times
Things go wrong sometimes
Vows are broken at times
Judas saw a lass
She looked like a native

The lass was lovely
The soldier was lonely
He tried his love lines
Alas! The lass gave him signs
She had her eyes on the soldier
So long she wished she was a gun
To be carried by the soldier

Sweet Samson disapproved

The illegal illicit affairs

Reminded soldier friend of the vows

Of the promises

Of the awaiting weddings

The temptation was high

The lass so sly

"It was just a kiss"

He retorted

The kiss graduated

To nights of carousal

The nights gave birth to

Months of rigorous romance

The soldier `danced

The soldier fought

Not the painful fight but

The fights of pleasure

Back in their hometown

The bride was waiting

Judas' bride was noble

Remained true to her word

But Samson' bride failed

She broke the vows

As Samson faithfully fought

His bride had a knight for nights

A stranger rode his favorite horse

Days went by

Nights ended so fast

It was count down

Waiting for the soldiers

To come back home

The war ended

Samson was excited

His hopes heightened

At the thought of his wedding

He didn't have the heart

To break the news

To the betrothed of his soldier friend

He pitied her

Back in hometown

Judas' beautiful bride

Walked in the air

Dreamt of love and kisses

She bought a bottle of wine

Adorned the house

To celebrate return of her betrothed

She pitied Samson

She lacked the heart

Of breaking news

That his bride had moved in

With the neighbor next door

Judas was boiling in love

The sly lass had Alas!

Given birth to a beautiful daughter

With Judas' eyes

He couldn't leave his empire

He carried his dynasty

He cared not

What awaited back home

Surprise awaited Samson

His bygone bride had nothing to hide

She was heavy

She had a heavy weight mate

Who took care of her

She had moved in with her beloved

And forgotten her betrothed

She cared not

About Samson's heart break

The long awaited day arrived

Soldiers had survived

Went straight to their houses

Judas with his dynasty

Opened the door

Thank God his betrothed was absent

Flowers welcomed him

He hid the card

Lied to his lovely lass

His parents had prepared for them

A surprise party

Samson arrived

With lovely long red roses

For his lovely bride

He found the door unlocked

His couches untouched

House quiet cold and abandoned

It hadn't been occupied for long

Scared and shocked

He dropped the gifts

Rushed to the neighbor next door

He run he hastened

To ask if they had seen his betrothed

He knocked at the door

Alas! Guess who opened?

His betrothed has changed

She has a big tummy

Behind her was heavy weight mate

Words failed him

As she banged the door

On his blank face

He went back

Picked the gun

An eye for an aye

Slowly he sighed

Suddenly he heard a lustrous yell

Hurried out to see

The voice was familiar

Hell had broken loose

Judas' bride had returned

Found the beautiful lass

With a beautiful kid

In the arms of her betrothed

Samson arrived in time

Looked at the devastated bride

Dangerously dying of pain

She saw him, her eyes red with fury

"Why didn't you tell me Samson?"

How could he tell her

He was dying inside?

In tears he replied

"Why didn't you tell me Tina

 That Terry had been taken?"

Suddenly she fainted

Fell in Samson's arms

There was no time to waste

The lass was watching

Her daughter cried

Judas held them tightly

Samson carried the jilted bride

To his abandoned house

It was first aid time

He wiped her tears

She regained consciousness

Reality hit harder

She had no words

The betrayal been big

Samson hid his gun

Postponed his revenge

He hugged her

She felt his arms

He wiped her tears

Tickled her cheeks

Laughter in the next room

Laughter and child chatter in the other

They looked at each other

Torrents of tears

Rolled down their cheeks

Damaged met damaged

Broken met broken

They studied each other's lips

As if to say

Hushhhh!!!!

PAINFUL PASSION©

To our standing soldiers

You may be a little broken

Slightly bruised

Permanently scarred

And sometimes betrayed

You may not be fully appreciated

Sometimes forgotten

And other times mistaken

I am talking of a soldier

Who slept in the bush last night

Protecting us from attackers

I am talking of a soldier

Who forgot the colour of his bed

With his degrees he chose the bush

Due to his love for his people

Listen to me darling

The risks cannot be paid

By any amount of money

The painful sacrifice

Look me in the eyes brother

I know you believe in eternal life

Coz brother

I cannot fathom

The great reward that awaits you

If the nights are quiet

The loneliness is loud

And the conditions cruel

Look up

See the stars

Choose the brightest star

It will be your hope

Do not lose it

It will bring you home

Let not the memory

Of your fallen brother

Engulf your mind

And blur your vision

Just let him go

It was his time to go

His painful sacrifice

Sent him direct to heaven

Focus on your star brother

Smile at the moon

You are a hero

A great hero

The best superstar

Your mother will welcome you home

Your father will say

`This is my son, whom I am proud of`

The lord will crown you

With the desires of your heart

You will settle down with your family

You will live long

And narrate to your grandchildren

The experiences at the bloody battle

The scary battle

You will be old

You will seat in a rocking chair

Next to your beautiful old lady

As you narrate your old fears

Your scary moments

You two will laugh at your

 Funniest moments in the bush

She will write a poem

Of the unsung hero

Grandson will tickle you from behind

You will stand attention

Hold imaginary gun and aim

Thinking it is the enemy

Once a soldier forever a soldier

Your grandchildren will

break into hysterical laughter

Your wife will join them

You will laugh the loudest

Don't lose your star brother

It will bring you home

You are the hero I know of

TRIBUTE TO BILLY©

What happened to you Billy?

Have always wondered really

How did you die?

Or is it just a lie?

Please talk to me Billy

I am worried really

This is my Billy's story

That makes my heart break

Nothing can reduce my worry

My chest as heavy as a brick

We met in a matatu

It was kitu saa tatu

We were strangers

Mixed up with villagers

Where are you Billy?

I am worried really

We were all depressed

Too hard to be impressed

We got out of the mat

We somehow got to talk

And for a while we did walk

I headed the other direction

We of course exchanged digits

Where are you Billy?

I am worried really

From then things weren't the same

You made communication an aim

Checking on me was duty

Though my heart was lame

Where are you Billy?

I am worried really

I learnt that you were in military

Based in Mogadishu solitary

You were on a leave

To search for your girlfriend

Who had given up your child

For adoption to a friend

You looked disturbed

Where are you Billy?

I am worried really

I had my problems too

Was one month pregnant

The man behind it gone forever

I didn't know what to do

The conditions were tough

The times were rough

I was on job search mission

Where are you Billy?

I am worried really

You called me often

You gave me a date before you left

The date was timely

We talked

We laughed

We shared

We gave each other hope

You told me never to give up

Especially on my child

Where are you Billy?

I am worried really

You called daily

You were consistent

Your texts were humorous

The pregnancy moved faster

Because of your night lengthy calls

We had a bond

Where are you Billy?

I am worried really

Distance never kept us apart

You still spoilt me

You came to see my son

Where he was three

Brought him beautiful bright clothes

You left by afternoon

I don't know what I saw in your eyes

You must have seen it in mine too

But no, my Billy was a gentleman

Where are you Billy?

I am worried really

Few days later

After return to Solitary Mogadishu

It remains a fearful fateful day

You called at midnight

You were not jovial

You sounded worried

For the 1st time you stammered

You didn't allow me to talk

You said there was no time

You talked as if in pain

The conversation is fresh in my mind

Where are you Billy?

I am worried really

"Hey, listen Mohana

I love you

I have always wanted

To walk down the aisle with you

To give you my name

To kneel down and ask you

To carry and mentor my children

Because you are noble

I wanted to hold your hand

Look you in the eye

Silence the storm

That took away your happiness

My heart bled when I saw you cry

I wanted to give you time

I was wrong, soldiers got no time

I can see your face as a grandma

Still beautiful at heart"

He talked too fast

Almost whispering

I tried to talk

He continued to talk

I said I loved him

He went off

I tried the phone

No one picked

Where are you Billy?

I am worried really.

I called him for months

The phone still quiet

One year ended

I sought him in the internet

Nowhere to be found

I sank deep into depression

Silently in solitude

Two years still no sigh

Where are you Billy?

I am worried really

Three years later

I tried calling

Your phone went through

My heart was racing

Adrenaline rising

A woman picked your phone

She didn't talk much

She asked who was calling

"I am Mohana, can I speak to Billy?"

Where are you Billy?

I am worried really

She was kind

She told me Billy was her brother

And he passed on 3years ago

I wanted to die

I cursed everything

I questioned God

I wanted to smoke anything

To drink my pain away

I headed to a club

I broke glasses

Fought with lasses

I broke my lenses

Why did you leave Billy?

I am frustrated really

Why didn't you say t'was time to die?

Why didn't you postpone death?

Why didn't you call me on death?

Why don't you appear to me?

Talk to me from the dead Billy

Why did you leave me alone?

You are a traitor

You promised to keep in touch

And to be happy

Why did you leave Billy?

I am frustrated really

I command you Billy listen to me well

You will not remain quiet

You got to talk to me tonight

The cold is tearing

The silence deafening

The solitude so striking

No other person understand me

I am a loner

I cannot even risk friendship

I am worried

Been left alone

No night phone calls

No flirty text

No sign of you

Where are you Billy?

I am worried really

You know something

I am still going

Sometimes I day dream

I see you and I

You emerge from somewhere

You tell me it was a mistake

Every time I am alone

You appear from the bush

Hold my tiny waist

Swing me around with those

Muscular soft hands

We dance

We laugh

As I am about to hug you

You disappear i clasp the air

My heart get tormented

You are too alive in my life

Where are you Billy?

I am sad really

Tempted to tell my son about you

But he cannot remember

Tears come down rolling

And he asks

"Why are you crying mummie?

I tell him my eyes are raining

Every time I think of you Billy

My eyes rain

I know you are happy Billy

I desperately miss you really

It is time to release you darling

The rare kind hearted soldier

Military life hadn't hardened thy heart

You were beautiful at heart

Handsome in appearance

Remember the day you held my hand in prayer?

We both cried

It was deep

It might have been our farewell

I still feel your hands tight on mine

I hear the moving prayer

You lie in peace

You sleep saintly

Sing serenity

Wherever you are Billy

I miss you really

To my heart you are alive

Though haven't really learnt

The art of mixing

Your departure gave me solitude

The emptiness is way too big

I wish I attended your funeral

I asked your sister

If I could visit your grave

She said No

That kills me Billy

And worries me really

You know what?

A lot has changed

I still look beautiful

My son is handsome

I definitely look pretty

Years are moving too fast

But something has changed

In my eyes you just see worry

Fear, mistrust and disillusionment

Unlike when I looked at you

The glow radiance in them gone

Life is hard

The struggles too tough

Times sickening rough

No one understands me

My eyes are raining again

Fare thee well Billy

People like you and me don't say bye

I will see you again Billy

I do miss you really.

Yours dearly Mohana

BATTLEFIELD AIN'T A SAFE VOYAGE©

It wasn't the best of times

It was time for war

It was tough

Leaving behind

A wife so beautiful

A gorgeous son

And a child unborn

Duty calls for the soldier

Many been devoured by the vulture

He gave them the last glance

Wondering if fate will give him a chance

To get another kiss

Took her by the waist and felt at ease

Kissed her like never before

Went down on his kneels

 Held the tiny hands of his heir

Amidst tears he mumbled

"Son, there comes a time

When loyalty to duty forces

One to make decisions so absurd

I may or may not come back

A soldier's life is like a leaf

The wind may blow it away

You may not understand now

But be a man enough

Take care of your mother

And your sibling once born"

The lieutenant commander was calling

The driver was hooting

`Don't be silly boy

 Battlefield ain't a safe voyage

Cut out damn promises

Tell her to prepare your funeral"

The brigadier general shouted

He wanted to curse him

But obedience no query was a rule

He looked at her

Tears rolled down their cheeks

The heir held the mother's hand

The soldier boarded the death truck

Colleagues patted his back

Saw his kingdom through the window

He parted his lips, he said

'I will come back home to you'

She parted her lips to say

'I love you I will wait for my soldier'

The truck veered off

He lost their trace

Battlefield is not a safe voyage

Many lost their arms

Many lost their lives

The soldier was at the front

His family portrait bound in his mind

The enemy was dangerous

Their weapons lethal

There was no time for retreat

The soldier had a duty

To slay the enemy

The enemy was a dragon

A faceted monster

The soldier saw

The brother at the front fall

The one on rear vomiting blood

The brother on his left dropped dead

The one on his right passed away

The soldier fought on

Back in his kingdom

The cold was too much

The loneliness too loud

Temptation too high

Queen of his kingdom too beautiful

The kingdom overthrown

A knight rode his horse

And fed his siblings

Secured his estates

Became the brother's keeper

The feeling was mutual

Too many years had gone by

For the queen to remember

The promise

The battlefield ain't a safe voyage

Yet some solders survive

Thanks to guardian angels and God

The soldier fought well

The soldier got the medal

And an approval from the lieutenant commander

The colonel said

"You are a brave soldier

You are an intelligent boy

You are major general Graham"

He took two steps

Saluted him

He wore the honor

And the medal

And the crown

The lieutenant saluted

The seniors envied him

It was time to go home

Home to the beautiful wife

The kids must have grown big

The party must be bigger

Than that of prodigal son

He had wounds

Soldiers don't return without wounds

But love will heal his wounds

The death truck veered via the forest

There lay bodies of slayed soldiers

Love kept him alive

He slept

He dreamt

Of the reunion

He was about to kiss her in the dream

When the driver shouted

"Brave boy life is a cycle

We are where we began

Go begin your life

Forget the slain heroes

Your maiden must be waiting

Your blood may not recognize you

But boy you are brave"

He looked at the death truck

They were two hundred soldiers in his squad

But he was the only one

Who came back

He remembered how they parted him

Now they were gone

Where no one returns

The death truck veered off

The driver waved goodbye

The compound hadn't changed much

The house looked radiant

He was Lucky to be home

He felt both happiness and fear

Sadness and joy intertwined

He stood at the spot he left

His wife, son and the unborn

As if they were still there

He walked to the door

Knocked thrice

A teenage girl opened the door

God! She resembled her mother

He smiled

Scared of the wounded soldier

She ran away

She came back in company

Of a young handsome man

Jeez! a copy of him in his twenties

They locked eyes

They seemed to communicate

But no !!!

The boy looked scared

No... worried!!

He looked at the portrait hanging

Yes the soldier is back

His blood seemed to know him not

He heard the familiar laughter

Coming from his bedroom

Yes he was excited

She was the one

She was his savior

She will introduce him to his own

He dropped his belongings

Run up stairs

His blood watched

He opened the door

"What ? Noooo….."

He shouted

A knight was riding his horse

She heard his voice

She looked

She saw the soldier

She tried to hide her nudity

Like Adam and Eve

After eating forbidden fruit

He stood there motionless

He saw the world go round

He needed not to be told

The kingdom had another king

He tried to talk

He was speechless

The soldier run down the stairs

Gave a look at his blood

Hit the road like a mad man

She run after him like a mad woman

The soldier was nowhere to be seen

He gulped down whiskey

He gulped down viceroy

He drank his pain away

He was about to take his life away

He was to drunk to reach the gun

He lied there wasted

They looked at her

They loathed her

They hated her

She was to blame

Who could understand?

The cold was too much

To wait for the soldier

The son looked at her with contempt

The mother-in-law hated her

People avoided her

She missed the soldier

Tears mixed with mucus and whiskey

She wanted to drink her pain away

In the dark she staggered

She found a wasted club house

She gulped down whiskey

She was too drunk

Men began making fun of her

They teased her

They harassed her

They were about to tear her dress

A gunshot was heard from behind

The soldier was fuming

With untold bitterness

He beat them all almost to death

He took her

She looked wasted

With her in his arms

He staggered away

Battlefield ain't a safe voyage

Their blood found them

In a drunken state

Listening to imaginary tango dance

SMILE AGAIN KATRINA ©

Happy was she before the news

Laughed heart out before her woes

She tumbled and tossed

With her gorgeous son as they played

When will Katrina smile again?

How could such news pass her by?

She hadn't gotten a wind

She had been playing with her lad

The breaking news broke her

When will Katrina smile again?

There had been a serious attack

In the camp where Kibby worked

It had happened in the dark

The soldiers were attacked

Majority left for the dead

When will Katrina smile again?

She checked the list

Her eyes full of mist

Here was among the dead

Luscious Kibby, Katrina's beloved

When will Katrina smile again?

She wanted to cry

She wanted to die

His son thought it was a lie

Down on the ground she lies

When will Katrina smile again?

With deep grieve mourned her sun

And forgot her son

She locked herself in her room

The breaking of things told her doom

When will you smile again Katrina?

The son sank into depression

Tried to get his mother's attention

Katrina never got out of her room

Your son needs you Katrina

When will you smile again?

She showed up during the burial

Her eyes had sunk deep into sockets

Her mind far away

She was really feeble

When will Katrina smile again?

She went back to her room

Broke glasses and whisky bottles

She fought inner battles

She was slowly losing her son

Smile to your son Katrina

Sam sat silently in a corner

His room was messy

He was drawing things

He didn't talk to anybody

Tears rolling down his cheeks

Sam needs you Katrina

She was about to do the worst

She served whisky

Poured poison in the same glass

She was tired

Your son is knocking Katrina

She looked at the glass

She cried

As she was about to drink

Her son shouted

"Open the door mum

I want to sleep next to you

Why do you hate me mum?"

He was sobbing

Come back to your senses Katrina

She rushed to open the door

Her son was there nose bleeding

She hadn't known

Her son was sick

It was not time to cry

It was first aid time

I'm sorry Katrina, take heart

The son is well now

The mother is still scared

She tells him she is sorry

The boy picks the glass

He says it is soda

Katrina hasn't seen yet

He is about to drink

Katrina kicks the glass

You almost killed your son Katrina

The boy is shocked

Mum has never been like this before

He runs to the door

Katrina is crying lying on the floor

Lying on broken glasses

The boy goes back

Stand up Katrina your son need you

Sam goes on his kneels

He utters in tears

'Get up mummie

Do not give up

All will be well

You need to eat something

You have become thin

It's okay Katrina put yourself together

She looks at her son

She smiles for the first time

She stands up

The boy hugs her

She tickles her son

He tickles her back

She says

"Come here small Kibby

We will get through this together'

The boy imitates the late dad

He says

"You look beautiful Mrs Kibby

Kibby misses you

But I love you more"

He tickles her

Alas Katrina is laughing again

FOR ALMOND

Alone in bed I lay, wondering which dragon to slay

I got a sad valentine, since I lost mine

Life's fragment lie, forgotten unseen I lie

Heart that truly loved gleams, petals of faded dreams

From hiding place he called, my eyes rolled

He promised we will meet, in love bed mate

The dead gone days I recall, when mists began to fall

I hear love's song of yore, in my heart dwells evermore

Your footsteps falter during the day, weary fade away

Life's dim shadows fall, like the sweetest song of all

When lights are low, your shadow softly come and go

You caress and cum inside, suddenly you hide

Which lover would not love, their beloved to have

Love thee with passion not put to use, that I had to lose

Love you in quiet need, as I water thy seed

By sun and by candlelight, my pains I fight

They call them fallen, their deaths so sudden

The surrender bidden, death road trodden

The wail of a mother, the tear of the father

Who will console the other, or wail they together

Lost and sad, frustrated and tired

The standing soldiers scared, almost mad

Remembering the battle so bloody, the fallen body

Their minds will never be steady, not any day

The fallen soldiers were hurt, others in pain sat

Who will heal the heart, full of but

The great doom, in our country loom

The hopes locked in tomb, to revert we ask whom

The soldiers wiped at noon, never lived to see moon

They thought they would fight on, gone were they soon

We cry and sigh, bleed inside as we say bye

To smile I try, while inside I die

With others you are gone, I feel so alone

Seems much like fate, I missed our date

I cannot dry mine eyes, nor do away with sighs

Baffled bitterly I try to get up again, my heart bargain

I am so deep in dust, more deep in dark

A creature may forget to weep, but mine so deep

I got too much fear, in my heart here

Old hope goes to the ground, your spirits around

The valentine rose, you gave me and chose

Like the spring bouquet adorned, suddenly abandoned

The blue forget-me-not, you gave as we tied knot

Adorned with ribbon stay, bright and gay

And fare -thee-well, my love and my well

Fare- thee- well, for a while

Will see you again and share champaign

In the next world

Bye Almond

In memory

Of

Him

Almond

BATTLE FIELD

While in the battle field
Remember not my kisses
For your kneels will be weak
The enemy will get your neck

While in the battle field
The soldier should not remember
Our dreams differed
For the bullet will blind you
And you will never dream again

While in the battlefield
Keep in the mid
Let bachelors take the front
And tired old ones at the rear
For their wives are tired
But my blood is hot
Waiting for the mid soldier
For those in the mid come home alive

While in the battle field
And they shoot your arm
Look not at corporal for approval
For he will never smile unless you are dying
Just remember my tender smile that I gave to you

When we first met at thc railway station
With your trouser torn at the rare

The pain will go
The arm will heal
The soldier will be on his feet
Fighting his way back to me
For my approval
And to the joy of an unborn son

While in the battle field
Fight well my soldier
For your pain my kisses will heal
And they will say
There is a new sheriff in town
See you soon my soldier

LAST DINNER WITH BILLY

His email had read that B was to arrive soon

After his deployment he always arrived afternoon

So I knew that soon I will have my love after longtime

One thing we had learnt was to treasure time

Being a soldier's girlfriend I knew on time we were powerless

So B would be calling any time to say he'll be home

My phone rung , my heart danced it was almost gloam

We had dated for three years but we kept it beneath

A soldier and a poet had to be sure before leaving underneath

But this time things were different we had studied each other

We had had all the explores we needed and trusted one another

We were to make arrangements on how to make relationship formal

We had kept it out of our relatives and friends it was normal

He had two days then I would be left to finalize arrangements

He was a soldier so my heart and body were used to abandonments

"Hey Jay I miss you like crazy will be home in an hour dress for dinner "

I can't explain how my heart felt , have you loved someone deep inner?

I loved B with love that made my whole being tremble at his voice

But above all ,Jeez ! His eyes ? I completely got lost in his eyes

The crystal clear ocean water made his eyes glow

His eyes were gateway to my world filled with stars and gleam

I hadn't known how joyous life was till I met Billy

My body was consumed by desire , I looked at his photo admiringly

I felt like my body was bursting with longing and excitement

He was calm and affectionate iced with fit toned chest arrangement

My spangly blue dress was splendidly sexy and effeminate

I had to look gorgeous , modest and elegant for my mate

Billy had a taste of style and this made him irresistible

Wore my make up but even without make up I was admirable

With my crop earing and pendant necklace I was good to go

The mirror whispered "You look glamorous miss you glow "

The dressed hugged my small curvy figure well

I arrived at **The Taste of Heaven diner restaurant** on time

Billy was watching a romantic pantomime

The setting was heavenly candle lit dinner was set for two

The sight was breathtaking particularly my lifetime boo

He turned around , our eyes locked , he rose my heart skipped

I don't know why we cried but no one spoke , tongues slipped

I looked into his eyes and I wished to be a tear and be there forever

"I missed you Jay , I missed my life for you are my life "

"I missed you B, I missed my life for it lies in your eyes "

We walked to the table , the music was alluring

The candle light was dazzling , scented romantic golden blue

The mood was right ,and here was my knight

We held hands, Nuzzled kissed and cuddled

We were to meet our parents in a month when B returns

We had very few hours of carousals

We went to heaven and came back

As we lay to rest his phone rang

He was to leave immediately

He looked at me his eyes were liquidly

I said I understood

We kissed

We shed tears

Our bodies wailed

He left

He was shot the following day

He was gone

BITTER SCARS

Inner wounds never heal nor can you seal

His mind was far far away waiting to decay

He stared at her and felt sorry not for himself but for her

Observed how worry had made her beauty fade, he was totally deranged

Once he is gone someone will take her, his bitterness and pain ranged

Soon he will be gone , will she be subject to pawn ?

His wounds had healed but inner ones were to kill him sooner

Before the war , he was not only a soldier but a popular crooner

He tried his voice but even his wheel chair seemed to laugh at him

Even in its crudest form sadness can't be this sad

She held the knife menacingly as she peeled off the potatoes

From where she was seated she could just tell his woes

She wondered how long it was going to be this way

Not having legs and arms wasn't as bad as not having emotions

His face had frozen and he was expressionless

The family and the military welfare had given up on him

She couldn't blame the welfare the country was not what it was before

It was a nation that drafted handsome soldiers to war without care

Those who came back wounded and' irreparable' were worse than the fallen

The media covered their compensation in millions but once it was over ,over it was!

She had laid her life down to take care of children while her soldier was serving nation

Right now he couldn't serve children , nation nor the desires of his woman

When other soldiers fell he didn't but he couldn't stand and she had to suffer need

Even in its crudest form sadness can't be this sad

She wondered how fast life changes and good things thrown to dogs

She was the top model years ago , a career she had to forego

Pain has a way of coming back and it hits where existed a crack

When she met Greg she was recovering from heartbreak

She remembered how Lenny had laid ugly model next to her in bed

Her heart sunk she had forgotten it but now she could hear their moans

He had said the best way to celebrate her success was drink to the fill

How could she tell the motive of the boyfriend she had dated for nine years ?

Greg was a demigod in entertainment industry

Girls screamed hysterically once he opened his mouth to sing

Glamour and demeanor oozed out of him !

She just fell for him in the midst of heart break

And a kiss sealed a deal

She remembered the kiss and her heart danced

But now her body had forgotten how it felt

Even in its crudest form sadness can't be this bad

Greg looked at Marylyn in dismay

He wanted to talk but he felt helpless

When he joined military he was sure to protect Lyn

In his mind the sounds of guns thundered

The blood of his friends splashed in front of him

He would scream aloud , by now Lyn was used to it

Torture ,torment , anguish distress and suffering

Were all written on his face already faceless

Before he got worse he had told Lyn to get married

But she refused and chose to take care of the injured

He remembered his hey days when he would step on stage

He remembered her heydays when she could hit the runways

A smile formed on his face ,but suddenly….

The guns begun again , the thunderous shots tore him to parts

The bleeding soldiers screamed as if consumed by hell fire

He advanced he saw a pool of blood and pain untold

His legs were a distance away , his arms couldn't be seen

He yelled, he cried ,he wailed

This time the scream scared Lyn who rushed to him

Even in its crudest form sadness can't be this sad

That night he slept for good

He saw peace at last

She stared at him , expressions of his face showed pain

She didn't know what to feel

The world cared not for the torture she underwent

Not only now but even when he was at the war

No one knew of the battles soldiers' wives fought

No one knew the dragons left for young widows to slay

No one knows they accompany their husbands in the bloody war

Marylyn just stared

Even in its crudest form sadness can't be this sad

Made in the USA
Columbia, SC
04 December 2019